DISCOVER BIOLOGY

Ecosystems

BY MARTHA LONDON

CONTENT CONSULTANT
BENJAMIN GOLLER, PhD
POSTDOCTORAL SCHOLAR
DEPARTMENT OF BIOLOGICAL SCIENCES
PURDUE UNIVERSITY

Kids Core
An Imprint of Abdo Publishing
abdobooks.com

abdobooks.com

Published by Abdo Publishing, a division of ABDO, PO Box 398166, Minneapolis, Minnesota 55439. Copyright © 2022 by Abdo Consulting Group, Inc. International copyrights reserved in all countries. No part of this book may be reproduced in any form without written permission from the publisher. Kids Core™ is a trademark and logo of Abdo Publishing.

Printed in the United States of America, North Mankato, Minnesota
052021
092021

Cover Photo: Andrey Armyagov/Shutterstock Images
Interior Photos: Odua Images/Shutterstock Images, 4–5; iStockphoto, 6, 12–13, 14, 18; Alessandro Zocc/iStockphoto, 7; Sarawut Kundej/Shutterstock Images, 9; Magalie St-Hilaire Poulin/Shutterstock Images, 10; Evan Austen/Shutterstock Images, 16; Peter Llewellyn/iStockphoto, 20–21; Richard Seeley/iStockphoto, 22; Kazakova Maryia/Shutterstock Images, 25; Shutterstock Images, 26, 29

Editor: Marie Pearson
Series Designer: Katharine Hale

Library of Congress Control Number: 2020948339

Publisher's Cataloging-in-Publication Data

Names: London, Martha, author.
Title: Ecosystems / by Martha London
Description: Minneapolis, Minnesota : Abdo Publishing, 2022 | Series: Discover biology | Includes online resources and index.
Identifiers: ISBN 9781532195310 (lib. bdg.) | ISBN 9781098215620 (ebook)
Subjects: LCSH: Biology--Juvenile literature. | Biotic communities--Juvenile literature. | Ecosystem management--Juvenile literature. | Life zones--Juvenile literature.
Classification: DDC 574.5--dc23

CONTENTS

CHAPTER 1
Everything Is Connected 4

CHAPTER 2
Nonliving Parts of an Ecosystem 12

CHAPTER 3
Living Parts of an Ecosystem 20

Picture Biology 28
Glossary 30
Online Resources 31
Learn More 31
Index 32
About the Author 32

Watering plants helps them grow.

Everything Is Connected

As the weather warms, Aimee watches how her backyard changes. Plants sprout in the soil. Soon flowers bloom. When the soil is dry, the plants start to droop. Rain helps them stand tall again.

Monarch butterflies drink nectar from flowers.

What Aimee loves most are the butterflies. Monarch caterpillars eat the milkweed in the garden. Aimee watches them build **chrysalises**. Butterflies break out of the hard shells. They flit

A ladybug eats insects that hurt plants.

from flower to flower. Aimee watches the butterflies drink the sweet **nectar** in the flowers.

Everything in Aimee's backyard is connected. Plants make sugar using sunlight and take **nutrients** from the soil. Insects eat the plants. Birds eat the insects. When plants and animals die, their remains put nutrients back into the soil. Aimee's backyard is an ecosystem.

What Is an Ecosystem?

An ecosystem is an area where living things interact with nonliving things. Plants, animals, soil, water, and air are all connected. Ecosystems can be huge. Or they can be very small. Areas with many similar ecosystems are called **biomes**. The ocean is an example of a biome. It has many smaller aquatic, or water-based, ecosystems in it.

Tide Pools

Oceans have tides. Water levels rise and fall over the course of the day. When the tide goes out, it leaves small ponds. These ponds are called tide pools. Tide pools are small ecosystems. High tide brings in plankton and algae that get energy from the sun. Animals in the tide pools eat these living things.

An ocean ecosystem can be home to many animals.

Animals such as raccoons have adapted to find food in cities.

The world is made up of many ecosystems. Healthy ecosystems are balanced. But they can become unbalanced. People can change an ecosystem. Sometimes people bring in plants and animals that do not typically live in an area.

These plants and animals may become invasive. They can crowd out **native** plants and animals.

People also build cities, farms, and roads. Sometimes plants and animals **adapt**. They can live alongside people. Other times, they cannot. These animals and plants may die. Many people work to protect ecosystems. People need healthy and balanced ecosystems for food and water.

Explore Online

Visit the website below. Does it give any new information about ecosystems that wasn't in Chapter One?

What Is an Invasive Species?

abdocorelibrary.com/ecosystems

Sunlight is an important part of an ecosystem.

CHAPTER **2**

Nonliving Parts of an Ecosystem

The nonliving parts of an ecosystem are called the abiotic parts. They include dirt, climate, water, and sunlight. Abiotic parts affect which plants and animals can live in an ecosystem.

Plants grow in soil with the right amount of nutrients.

Something in the Soil

Soil is an important part of an ecosystem. Soil has nutrients. Nutrients come from different sources. One source is minerals in rocks. Dead animals are another source. As the animals **decompose**, nutrients from their bodies return to the soil.

These nutrients allow plants to grow. If there are not enough nutrients, plants can die.

Similarly, if soils have the wrong kinds of nutrients, then plants do not have what they need to grow.

Climate

A place's climate is its typical weather over time. Some places are warm. Others are cold. Still other places have both hot and cold seasons. Plants and animals are adapted to the temperatures of their ecosystems. They cannot live in ecosystems that have very different temperature ranges.

Some ecosystems are sunny. Others are cloudy. Some plants need lots of sun. Others grow better in cloudy places.

Rain forests get a lot of rain.

Some places get high winds. They knock down big trees so new plants can grow. But some plants cannot survive in windy locations. They need calmer places.

Water

Animals and plants need water to survive. Some ecosystems, such as lakes, have a lot of water. Others are very dry. Desert ecosystems have almost no liquid water. Some forests get a lot of rain. Rain forests are named for their wet climates. Other forests are dry. Plants and animals have adapted to the water available in their ecosystems.

Solar Energy

One important part of ecosystems is sunlight. Plants need sunlight. They use energy from the sun for photosynthesis. This is the process of using the sun's energy to make sugar. The plant can use this sugar or store it. Photosynthesis, along with water and soil, helps plants grow.

Cactuses survive in the desert by storing water.

In dry places, some plants store water in their roots and leaves. Desert animals may get the water they need from what they eat. When it rains, deserts bloom with bright flowers. Plants take in as much water as they can.

Primary Source

Researcher Rick Haney talks about how using too many chemicals in farming can hurt the soil. In an interview, Haney said:

> We are destroying the [plant and animal remains] in the soil, and we've got to bring that back to sustain life on this planet.

Source: Richard Schiffman. "Why It's Time to Stop Punishing Our Soils with Fertilizers." *Yale Environment 360*, 3 May 2017, e360.yale.edu. Accessed 9 July 2020.

Comparing Texts

Think about the quote. Does it support the information in this chapter? Or does it give a different perspective? Explain how in two to three sentences.

Birds rely on plants and animals in an ecosystem for food.

CHAPTER 3

Living Parts of an Ecosystem

The abiotic parts of an ecosystem support the living, or biotic, parts. Plants and animals make up the living parts of an ecosystem. Biotic and abiotic parts of an ecosystem rely on one another.

Foxes depend on dirt to dig shelters.

Plants and Animals

Plants and animals need abiotic parts of an ecosystem. Rain, soil, and sunlight are important for plants. Plants get the nutrients they need from water and air. They use energy from sunlight to turn the nutrients into energy the plants can use to grow. Animals need water too. They need to drink it. Some animals also need to live in water. And some need dirt so they can dig shelters.

Three Ecosystems in One

A tropical rain forest is an example of a biome. Biomes have more than one ecosystem in the same area. Some scientists divide rain forests into three ecosystems. The canopy is at the top. The understory is beneath it. At the bottom is the forest floor. Each area has specific plants and animals that live there.

Plants and animals also need each other. Animals such as bats and bees **pollinate** many types of flowers and trees. Pollination allows plants to make seeds and fruits. Then more plants can grow.

Plants provide food for insects and other animals, including humans. People eat foods such as bananas and lettuce. Many types of insects eat plants.

Insects also eat other insects. Larger animals such as mice eat insects too. Even larger animals eat the mice. A food web illustrates these connections. It shows how energy from the sun travels from one living thing to another.

Parts of an Ecosystem

This image shows an example of a pond ecosystem. Some parts are living, and other parts are nonliving.

Some mushrooms break down dead trees into nutrients.

Eventually, all plants and animals die. Their remains contain nutrients. Animals such as worms and termites help break down the remains. Decomposers such as fungi also help break down dead things. They return nutrients to the soil. New plants take in those nutrients.

A balanced ecosystem provides food and shelter to living things. Living things rely on each other and abiotic parts to survive. Everything in an ecosystem is connected and plays an important role.

Further Evidence

Look at the website below. Does it give any new evidence to support Chapter Three?

Habitats and Ecosystems

abdocorelibrary.com/ecosystems

Picture Biology

There are living and nonliving things in an ecosystem. What living things do you see in this photo? What nonliving things do you see? What examples can you find of living and nonliving things interacting?

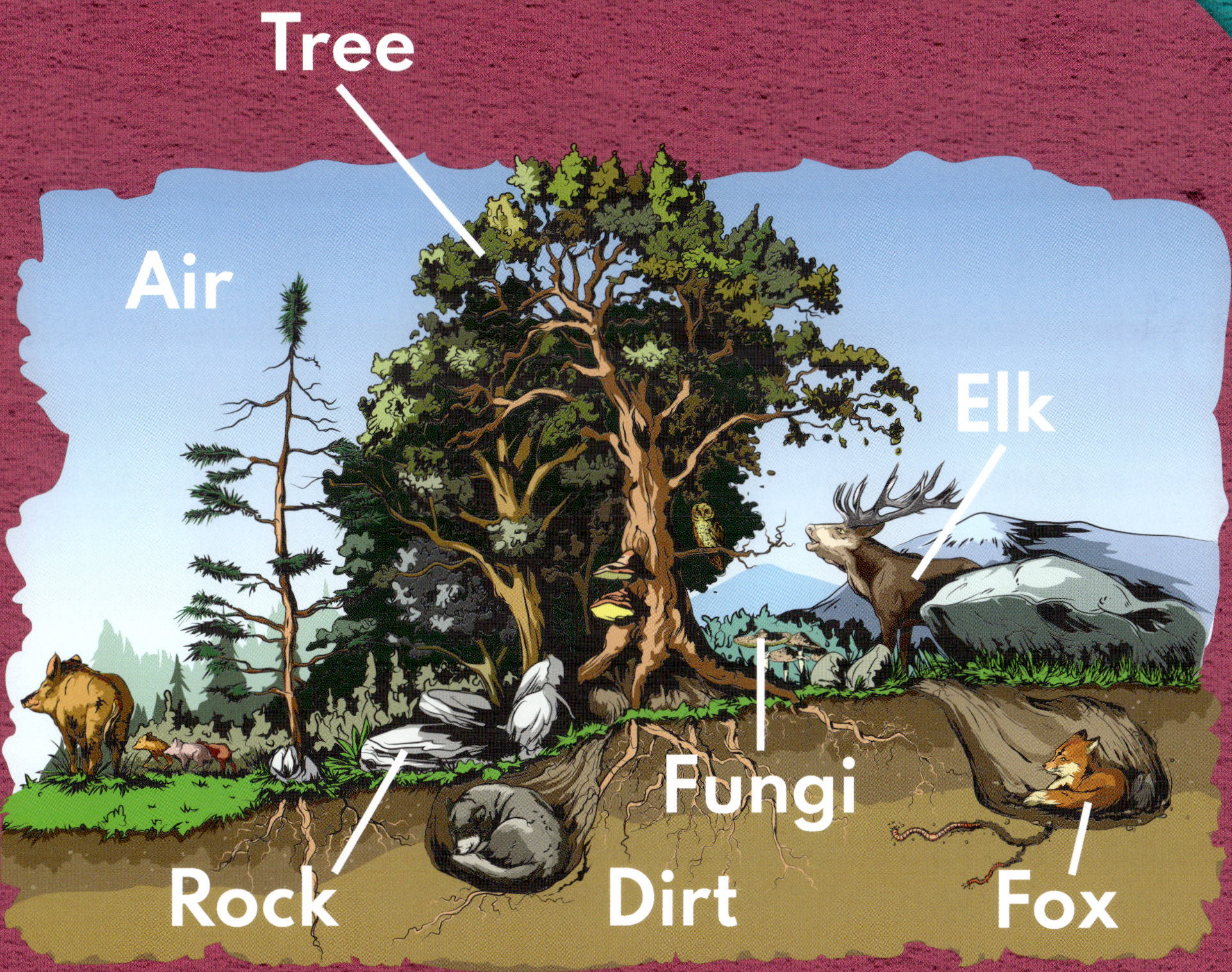
Tree
Air
Elk
Fungi
Rock
Dirt
Fox

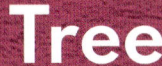

Glossary

adapt
to change as a species to survive in a certain place

biomes
areas with more than one ecosystem

chrysalises
hard cases that protect caterpillars as they turn into butterflies

decompose
to break down into simpler pieces

native
naturally occurring in a place

nectar
sweet liquid in a flower

nutrients
substances living things need in order to survive

pollinate
to spread pollen from one plant to another so the receiving plant can make seeds

Online Resources

To learn more about ecosystems, visit our free resource websites below.

Visit **abdocorelibrary.com** or scan this QR code for free Common Core resources for teachers and students, including vetted activities, multimedia, and booklinks, for deeper subject comprehension.

Visit **abdobooklinks.com** or scan this QR code for free additional online weblinks for further learning. These links are routinely monitored and updated to provide the most current information available.

Learn More

Huddleston, Emma. *Food Chains*. Abdo Publishing, 2022.

Milner, Charlotte. *The Rainforest Book*. DK Children, 2021.

Petersen, Christine. *Study Soils*. Abdo Publishing, 2020.

Index

animals, 7–11, 13–15, 17–18, 19, 21–26

biomes, 8, 23
butterflies, 6–7

climate, 13, 15, 17

decomposers, 14, 27
dirt, 13, 23

food, 11, 24, 27

living parts, 8, 21, 25, 27

nonliving parts, 8, 13, 25
nutrients, 7, 14–15, 22–23, 26–27

plants, 5, 7–11, 13–18, 21–27

rain, 5, 17–18, 22
rain forests, 17, 23

sunlight, 7, 13, 15, 17, 22–23

tide pools, 8

water, 8, 11, 13, 17–18, 22–23

About the Author

Martha London lives and works in Minnesota. She writes books for young readers full-time. When Martha isn't writing books, you can find her hiking in the woods or snuggled up with her cat.